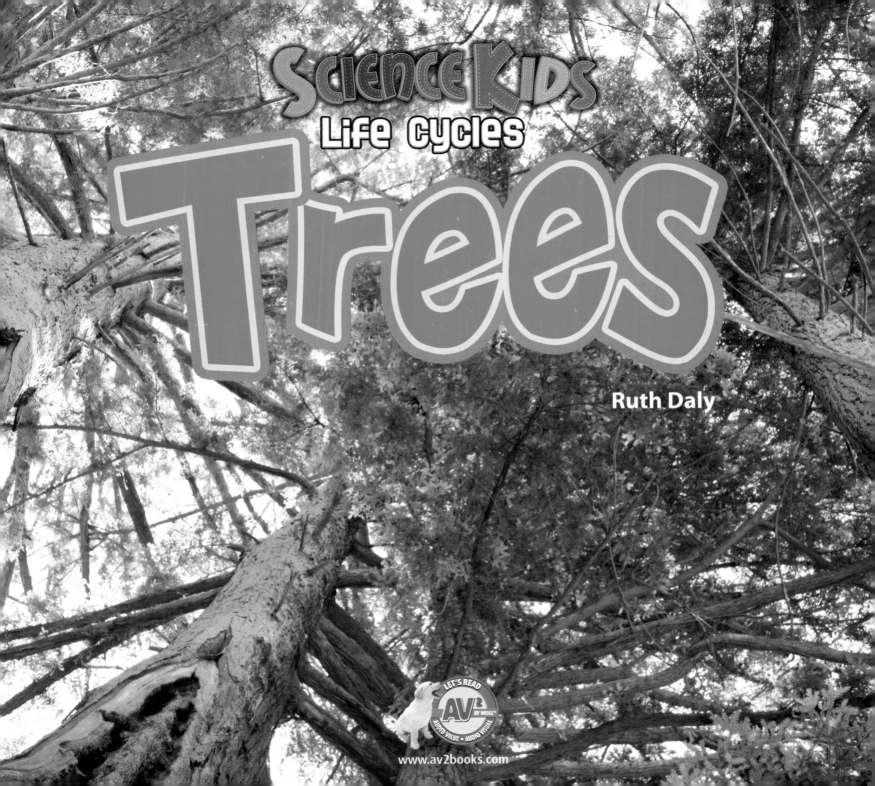

Science Kids
Life Cycles
Trees

Ruth Daly

AV² provides enriched content that supplements and complements this book. Weigl's AV² books strive to create inspired learning and engage young minds in a total learning experience.

Your AV² Media Enhanced books come alive with...

Audio
Listen to sections of the book read aloud.

Video
Watch informative video clips.

Embedded Weblinks
Gain additional information for research.

Try This!
Complete activities and hands-on experiments.

Key Words
Study vocabulary, and complete a matching word activity.

Quizzes
Test your knowledge.

Slide Show
View images and captions, and prepare a presentation.

... and much, much more!

Go to **www.av2books.com**, and enter this book's unique code.

BOOK CODE

S21518

AV² **by Weigl** brings you media enhanced books that support active learning.

Published by AV² by Weigl
350 5th Avenue, 59th Floor New York, NY 10118
Websites: www.av2books.com   www.weigl.com

Library of Congress Control Number: 2014941060

ISBN 978-1-4896-1338-7 (hardcover)
ISBN 978-1-4896-1339-4 (softcover)
ISBN 978-1-4896-1340-0 (single user eBook)
ISBN 978-1-4896-1341-7 (multi-user eBook)

Printed in the United States of America in North Mankato, Minnesota
1 2 3 4 5 6 7 8 9 0   18 17 16 15 14

052014
WEP220514

Project Coordinator: Jared Siemens
Art Director: Terry Paulhus

Weigl acknowledges Getty Images as the primary image supplier for this title.

SCIENCE KIDS
Life Cycles

Trees

CONTENTS

4

All trees begin life, grow, and make more trees. All trees will die in the end. New trees grow up to take their place. This is a life cycle.

Trees are the biggest plants on the Earth. They have wooden trunks and branches. Trees grow leaves or needles on their branches.

7

8

Trees begin life as seeds. Seeds are very small. They have food stored inside to help them grow.

Seeds grow roots in the ground. These roots find water for the tree.

A sprout soon breaks through the shell of the seed. It pushes through the soil into the air. Sprouts need soil, light, and water to help them grow.

11

The stem grows stronger. It also changes color. This is the seedling stage of the life cycle. A seedling has thin bark and a few leaves.

13

A seedling becomes a sapling when its trunk grows thicker. Leaves grow on its branches. Leaves use energy from the Sun to make food for the tree.

Most adult trees have flowers or cones. Flowers make pollen. Flowers need their pollen moved from one part of the flower to another. Insects and wind help the flower move its pollen. This helps flowers make fruit.

Some seeds grow in fruit. Seeds can make more trees when fruit falls off the tree. Seeds are sometimes moved by the wind, water, or animals. This helps trees grow in other places.

There are many different kinds of trees. Each kind of tree has different leaves and fruit. A seed will grow into the same kind of tree as the one it came from.

Life Cycles Quiz

Test your knowledge of tree life cycles by taking this quiz. Look at these pictures. Which stage of the life cycle do you see in each picture?

adult   seed
seedling   flowering
sprout   sapling

23

KEY WORDS

Research has shown that as much as 65 percent of all written material published in English is made up of 300 words. These 300 words cannot be taught using pictures or learned by sounding them out. They must be recognized by sight. This book contains 73 common sight words to help young readers improve their reading fluency and comprehension. This book also teaches young readers several important content words, such as proper nouns. These words are paired with pictures to aid in learning and improve understanding.

Page	Sight Words First Appearance
5	a, all, and, grow, end, in, is, life, make, more, new, place, take, the, their this, to, trees, up, will
6	are, Earth, have, leaves, on, or, plants, they
9	as, find, food, for, help, small, them, these, very, water
11	air, help, into, it, light, of, soon, through
12	also, changes, few, has
15	from, its, use, when
16	another, most, move, one, part
19	animals, by, can, off, other, some, sometimes
20	came, different, each, kinds, many, same, there

Page	Content Words First Appearance
5	life cycle
6	branches, needles, trunks
9	ground, roots, seeds
11	shell, soil, sprout
12	bark, color, seedling, stage, stem
15	energy, sapling, Sun
16	adult, cones, flowers, fruit, insects, pollen, wind

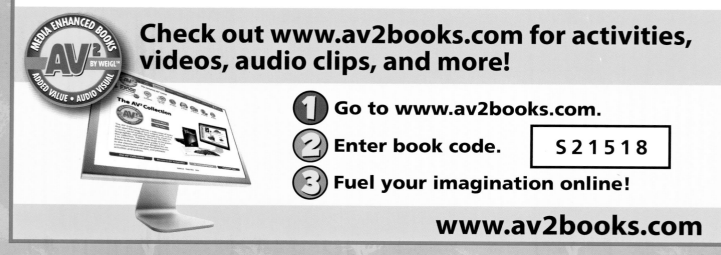